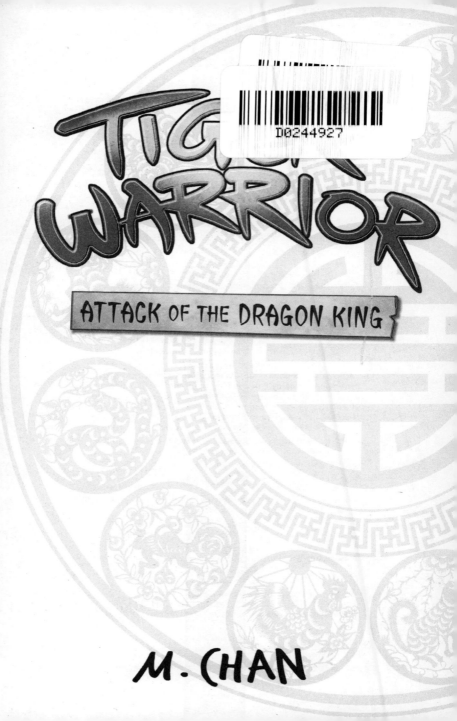

TIGER WARRIOR

ATTACK OF THE DRAGON KING

M. CHAN

For Kairen, a warrior in the making

Thanks to Inclusive Minds for introducing us to Anna Loo through their network of Inclusion Ambassadors.

ORCHARD BOOKS

First published in Great Britain in 2021 by Hodder & Stoughton Limited

7 9 10 8 6

Text © Orchard Books Ltd 2021
Cover and inside illustrations by Alan Brown, represented by Advocate Art, © Orchard Books Ltd 2021

A CIP catalogue record for this book is available from the British Library.

ISBN 978 1 40836 308 9

Printed in Great Britain

MIX
Paper from
responsible sources
FSC® C104740

The paper and board used in this book are made from wood from responsible sources

Orchard Books
An imprint of Hachette Children's Group
Part of Hodder & Stoughton Limited
Carmelite House, 50 Victoria Embankment, London EC4Y 0DZ

An Hachette UK Company
www.hachette.co.uk
www.hachettechildrens.co.uk

CONTENTS

Prologue 5

Chapter One 13

Chapter Two 25

Chapter Three 39

Chapter Four 53

Chapter Five 69

Chapter Six 87

Chapter Seven 105

Chapter Eight 121

Chapter Nine 131

PROLOGUE

The huge lion beast stretched out its giant claws. Next to it, a nine-tailed fox pounced. The Dragon King put his hands behind his back and smiled as he walked past the paintings. There was probably a picture of him here somewhere. Once he had been the most powerful monster of them all.

He hid his smile as he approached the throne and knelt before the Jade Emperor. "Thank you for letting me out to speak to you, Your Celestial Majesty," he said. "I have been imprisoned under the Mystic Mountain for ten long years. I have had time to think, and I want to beg your forgiveness, and to be your second in command again."

The Jade Emperor smiled. "We were friends once. We can be again."

"That's exactly what I want," said the Dragon King, allowing himself a small smile as he stood up. The Jade Emperor led him down a grand hallway lined with priceless vases and silk tapestries, into his private chamber. He sat down at the table, which was laid for tea, and then bowed, indicating that the Dragon King could sit. But the Dragon King did not.

Instead he stood tall, clapping his hands together in a thunderous bang. A flash blinded the Jade Emperor and his two guards shielded their eyes. The Dragon King transformed into his gigantic dragon form, roaring as power surged through his now snake-like scaly body, his tail unfurled, his claws extended. After all this time, the Dragon King had his power back!

He swung his tail, knocking out both the guards in one swift move. The Jade

Emperor rolled out of the way. With his opponent on the floor, the Dragon King swooped down to attack again. The Jade Emperor blasted a beam of light from his hands into the dragon's side, but although the light crackled and burned his flesh, the huge dragon only paused for a second.

"Give up now! You know you can't beat me," the emperor said.

"Never!" roared the Dragon King,

flinging the Jade Emperor into a corner.
"It's different this time. I have a power so
great that I can finally defeat you!"

The Dragon King waved one eagle-
like claw in a circle, and a green staff
appeared in the room. He pointed it at
the Jade Emperor.

"The Jade Staff!" cried the Jade
Emperor. "But how? How did you get it?"

"Many dragons died bringing this to
me," the Dragon King snarled. "But it will
be worth it to defeat you!" He pointed
the staff at the Jade Emperor again, and
in an instant, the emperor was gone.

The Dragon King looked out of the
window at a huge snow-topped mountain

and laughed, knowing that the emperor was deep beneath it in a tiny cell. The Jade Emperor was now *his* prisoner. With a wave of his claw he transformed back into his human body, holding the staff aloft.

"The Jade Kingdom is finally mine!" he proclaimed.

CHAPTER ONE

"Take that!" Jack yelled. He pressed the buttons on his controller and the game's green dragon exploded in a splatter of dust. But just as Jack thought he had won, an orange dragon flew out of a castle and began to attack his avatar.

"Oh, no you don't!" His avatar rolled away from the dragon's flames. "That was close!"

Jack's bedroom door opened and his grandpa, who he called Yeye, came in. He stood by the door, watching Jack playing his game. "Hi, Yeye," Jack said, not taking his eyes from the screen.

"That's not how to defeat a dragon," Yeye said.

"Oh, yeah?" Jack laughed, twisting around in his gaming seat to look at Yeye, whose eyes were shining mischievously.

"Do it like this!" Yeye sprang up, kicking hard, his slipper flying into the air and almost knocking Jack's lamp over. Jack's jaw dropped. "And then turn ... like this ... uppercut!" Yeye yelled as he punched into the air with surprising ferocity.

Jack grinned then swivelled back round
to his screen. He pushed the buttons, trying
to copy Yeye's moves. His avatar leapt,
punching the red dragon into oblivion.

"No way! It worked!" Jack turned to see

Yeye bent over, coughing as he made his way to Jack's chair.

"Yes! I told you!" Yeye said, taking breaths in between coughs.

Jack got up and went to his grandpa, whose face was going beetroot red.

"Shall I get some water?" Jack asked.

"No, don't worry about me. Just got something in my throat," Yeye choked out. "I'm fine."

Yeye didn't look fine. "I think you should rest," Jack said. "You're always saying you're not a spring chicken any more!"

"This old chicken could outrun you any day!" Yeye joked, stifling more coughs.

"But I think it's time, Jack ..."

"Time for what?" Jack asked, helping his grandpa to sit down.

"To pass on to you something which was Ju-Long's."

"Dad's?" Jack said in surprise.

Yeye nodded. "Which was your father's before he ..."

"Before he died." Jack sat down next to his grandad. "Yeye, is everything OK?" His grandpa was acting really strangely.

"Jack, are you brave enough to face a real dragon?" Yeye asked, looking deadly serious.

"There's no such thing! Yeye, I think you need to rest." Jack laughed.

"I'm serious ... I'm not going to be around for ever. It's time." Yeye grabbed hold of his arm. "Come to my room; I've got something special I need to give you. Before it's too late."

"OK, you're scaring me now." Why was his granddad acting so weird? Jack always felt a little knot in his belly when Yeye mentioned his dad. He'd died when Jack was one. Not long afterwards, Yeye had decided to move from China and come and live with Jack and his mum.

Jack shook his head as he followed Yeye to his room across the landing.

"Come! You will see!" Excitedly now, Yeye shuffled into his bedroom. Jack loved Yeye's room. It smelled tangy from his ointment, and the walls were covered in long scrolls with brush art pictures of dragons, as well as funny cartoons Yeye had cut out from newspapers. Yeye noticed Jack looking around. "Your father would have been happy that you were going to have it ..." Yeye pulled out a wooden box and opened it slowly. He held something in the palm of his hand, which he extended to Jack. "This is for you."

"Thanks, I guess ..." said Jack, taking the shiny pale green disc and turning it over.

Yeye reached out and cuffed Jack's ear.

"Oww!" Jack yelled. "What's that for?"

"Thanks, I guess? That was for your cheeky monkey talk. This is the Jade Coin, the most precious object in the universe!" Yeye looked different now, his face radiant as he gazed at the green thing in Jack's hand. "Look closely. What can you see?"

"Well ..." Jack said. He stared hard at the coin – he recognised the twelve creatures of the zodiac. Yeye had drilled into him the story of the animals and how they came to be in the Chinese Zodiac, and every bedtime he would tell Jack a different myth. "OK, so yeah, I see.

The Rat, Ox, Tiger, Rabbit, Dragon, Snake,
Horse, Goat, Monkey, Rooster, Dog, Pig ...
see, I was listening."

"Good!" Yeye chuckled. "I was going
to wait until you were older, but you
are right. I am no spring chicken – more
like an old goose. I taught you about the
ancient myths for a reason."

"To bore me to death?" Jack said,
ducking before Yeye could cuff him again.

"Listen. Jack ... I have something
to tell you." Yeye held his grandson's
shoulders and stared into his eyes. "You
are the Tiger Warrior! You must take up
your place and battle the forces of evil in
the Jade Kingdom."

Yeye paused dramatically. Jack rolled his eyes.

"If demons take over the Jade Kingdom, then our world will be next!" Yeye said urgently.

Jack laughed. "Yeah right, good one, Yeye!"

"I see that I'm going to have to convince you," Yeye said. With a quick flick of his fingers, he tossed the Jade Coin into the air. As it spun, it caught the light, filling Yeye's bedroom with colourful rainbows. It seemed almost … magical.

"TIGER TRANSFORM!" Yeye shouted out loud. In a flash, he disappeared. And in his place was a huge, roaring tiger!

CHAPTER TWO

There was a giant tiger in his grandpa's bedroom. Jack wanted to run but his feet were frozen to the spot. The tiger looked at him and its shoulders moved as if it was laughing.

"Yeye? Is that you?" Jack asked. The tiger nodded its head.

"How did you do that?" Jack exclaimed in amazement.

In a flash, Yeye was back to his old self. But his coughing was even worse than before. He stumbled over to the door frame and leant on it before flicking the magic Jade Coin into the air once more.

"ZODIAC!" he shouted. All of a sudden, the room was crammed full of animals, each one glowing with a different coloured light. Monkey was swinging from the dusty beige lampshade. Rabbit hopped across Yeye's floor. Dog was making himself comfy on the bed and next to him Pig was smelling the air. Rooster was on top of the wardrobe, bobbing his head

backwards and forwards. Tiger was by the window, half-hidden by the curtains.

"Well, if it wasn't about time. My body is so tightly wound up!" Snake said as she slithered over towards Jack's feet.

"I get to meet him first as I am number one of the zodiac," said Rat as she scurried over the headboard and sniffed at Jack's arm.

"First but tiny." Tiger growled. "I want to greet him first. He's the Tiger Warrior, after all ..." Tiger padded over and rubbed his head on Jack's leg. Jack looked down, not knowing whether to pat the huge beast or not.

"Cock-a-doodle-doo!" Rooster called.

"OK! OK! Everyone, calm down! You'll all get a chance to meet him, and so will the others," said Yeye.

Jack glanced around. Of course, there were twelve zodiac animals, so a few were missing: Goat, Horse, Ox and Dragon. Jack felt a thrill of excitement about meeting a real dragon.

"Jack, these are the animals of the zodiac. They are contained by the magic of the Jade Coin, but they can come out whenever they want. Sometimes it's most inconvenient ..."

"Yeah, like when we come out when you're asleep," snorted Pig.

"Or in the loo!" shouted Dog.

"Baaaa ... tell him that he can call on us too," added Goat from the doorway. Yeye ushered her in and shut the door, making the room even more cramped.

"The Tiger Warrior has the power to summon the animals and use their powers," Yeye explained. "And when you have unlocked their skills ... then you will be able to transform into one of them. Like I just did with Tiger."

"This is all completely crazy," Jack said in disbelief. "I'm not a warrior, I'm just an ordinary kid."

Yeye looked into Jack's eyes. "Jack, there is nothing ordinary about you."

Jack wasn't so sure.

"Can I show him what I can do?" Snake asked.

Yeye nodded and Snake began to slither around Jack's right arm. He tried not to panic that he had a snake on him. Snake smiled in a friendly way. As soon as she was coiled around his arm, she shut her eyes and Jack's arm started to pulse with energy. He felt a strange melting sensation run through his body. He glanced down at his feet – but they weren't there anymore.

"Look." Yeye pointed to his mirror.

But Jack couldn't see himself. He was invisible! And so was Snake, even though he could still feel her wrapped around his arm. It was incredible!

"Awesome! I can use this to sneak up on my friends at school."

"No, it's not a game. We don't take them to school," Yeye said fiercely.

Snake unfurled and slowly she and Jack reappeared. "Shame, I would have liked to have gone to sssssschool," she said, flickering her forked tongue.

"What other things can they do, Yeye?" Jack said, eager for more magic powers to be revealed.

"Dragon controls water, Ox has super

strength, Rat influences the weather ..."

"If you need a tornado, I'm your rat,"
Rat scurried on to the top of Dragon's
head to get a better view.

"What about Goat?" Jack asked. *I bet
it's something boring,* he thought.

"No need to be rude!" said Goat.

"What?" Jack said, feeling confused.
He hadn't said anything.

"She is telepathic, Jack, she can read
people's minds. Apologise, please," Yeye
said. "We don't want to get off on the
wrong hoof."

Jack bent down and looked Goat in the
eye. "Sorry, I didn't mean to hurt your
feelings. And your power is really cool!"

"Baaaa, apology accepted. And yes …
I can see what you are wondering." Goat
turned to Yeye. "He wants to know why
he's called the Tiger Warrior and not the
Rooster Warrior, or Pig Warrior …"

"She's right!" Jack exclaimed.

"Monkey Warrior has a better ring to it
if you ask me," joked Monkey.

"What year of the zodiac were you
born in, Jack?" asked Yeye.

"Year of the Tiger," Jack told him.

"Correct, just like your dad. Just like
me. And my mother before me, and
throughout the generations all the way
back to the first Tiger Warrior. We're
always the keepers of the coin. It's

because we have the heart of a tiger," said Yeye patting his chest. Tiger nodded his head. "Your job as Tiger Warrior is to protect the Jade Kingdom," said Yeye.

"It's in the next realm," added Snake.

Jack sat down on the bed, shaking his head. It was all so much to take in: the magic, the animals ... Dog came and sat on his lap and Jack felt himself relax. "Slow down, what's the Jade Kingdom?" he asked.

"It's like this, Jack," said Pig, snuffling at a bowl of mints on Yeye's bedside table. "Imagine this is the Jade Kingdom. Demons want to destroy it, like this—" Pig put his nose in the sweet bowl.

"Pig!" yelled Tiger. "You just want to eat the sweets!"

"What?" said Pig, munching away. "I was hungry."

"It's about saving the world," said Yeye. He sat down next to Jack and looked at him earnestly. "Demons, dragons and all kinds of creatures from the spirit realm want to take over the Jade Kingdom and, if they do, then our world will be next."

"But nothing cool has happened for ages," sighed Rat. "I've been itching for a battle; it's been too long."

"That's just your fleas!" Dog laughed as Rat leapt at him.

"Things have been peaceful in the Jade Kingdom since I imprisoned the Dragon King under the Mystic Mountain, ten years ago," Yeye said proudly. "Your father took over from me as the Tiger Warrior. But when he died you were far too young to take his place, so I had to become the Tiger Warrior again, even though I was already past my prime."

Jack felt that knot in his belly again. He wished his dad were here to tell him what to do. Jack didn't feel brave or strong. He couldn't even do ten press-ups.

"I know that you have doubts, Jack. But I'm telling you that YOU are the only choice." said Yeye, pushing himself up from the bed. "Now stand up."

Jack slowly did as Yeye asked. Quietly, the animals lined up and faced him.

"Take the coin," Yeye said, sounding solemn. Yeye held one side of the Jade Coin and Jack took the other. As he did, Jack saw it glow brightly.

Jack's hands began to feel warm, then hot as energy surged into them, swirling with magical power. "You are now the Tiger Warrior!" boomed Yeye.

Yeye let go of the coin. It was in Jack's hands now. And so, if he believed Yeye, was the fate of the world.

CHAPTER THREE

Jack felt every muscle in his body surge with magical energy.

"Quickly, change into a tiger!" Yeye urged him.

Jack stood tall and closed his eyes. Holding his breath, he flipped the coin. "TIGER TRANSFORM!" he shouted, just as Yeye had before. He opened one eye to see if anything had happened. But his very human hand was still outstretched. He wiggled his fingers. Still nothing. He opened both eyes and looked at Yeye, who was holding his belly. At first Jack thought he was in pain, but then he saw the tears of laughter streaming from Yeye's eyes.

"Ha ha ha! That was so funny! I haven't had such a good laugh in a long time! You should have seen your face, all scrunched up, thinking it would work first time."

"Yeye!" said Jack, feeling his face getting warmer and probably redder. He should have known Yeye would still be playing jokes on him – he could never stay serious for long.

"Listen, one day you will have the power within yourself to transform into each of the zodiac animals, but it does not come easily. You have to train hard. You have to understand the tiger's spirit, not with this ..." Yeye gently touched Jack's head "... but with this ..." and he patted Jack's chest. "Heart. When your spirit aligns with the animal, then and only then will you be able to fully harness its power. Until then, you'll have to be touching the animals to use their power."

"I'll try my best, Yeye," said Jack looking down at the coin.

"Come, you should go to the Jade Kingdom. Go see for yourself the world that is beyond our eyes and senses. It's truly magical, Jack – you will love it." Yeye took the coin from Jack and flicked it as if he were going to click his fingers. "Jade Kingdom!" he announced.

The coin spun in mid-air. It whirled around and around. The light moved in circular motions like a Catherine wheel, growing bigger and bigger until it was big enough to step through. Jack's mouth hung open. The space in the centre of the circle was no longer Yeye's bedroom. Jack could see beautiful green hills and tall red houses like the ones he'd seen in

Yeye's books.

"Go through, Jack." Yeye plucked the coin out of its suspended state in the air and gave it to Jack. "Go and show this to the Jade Emperor; he will know you are the new Tiger Warrior.

When you want to come back, flick the coin and say 'HOME'."

Jack stepped closer to the portal, then turned.

"Aren't you coming too?" Jack said, looking at his grandpa's face, trying to figure out why the old man wasn't moving.

Yeye shook his head sadly. "I can't. Only the Tiger Warrior can enter the Jade Kingdom. You go ahead. Enjoy your time there, eat the most delicious foods you will ever taste and marvel at the most wonderful creatures you will ever see. You will recognise some things from the stories I have told you." He sighed.

"I'm afraid that I can never return."

"But Yeye—" Jack shuffled his feet nervously.

"There's nothing to worry about. The kingdom has been at peace since I imprisoned the Dragon King. I'll start training you later, but for now go and enjoy yourself. Find the Jade Emperor, show him the coin and send my regards. Go now, you'll be home before your mum gets home from work. Time passes differently there."

"All right then," Jack said, trying not to feel too nervous. "But I'm just going to have a quick look around. I'll introduce myself to the Jade Emperor and then I'm coming straight back." He looked at Yeye, not wanting to leave him behind. He'd not been anywhere on his own before, never mind a different magical world.

"Trust me, you'll have a brilliant time. Now go! And while you're gone I may or may not have a little snooze," said Yeye.

"OK, I can do this," Jack muttered to himself, and stepped through the whizzing circle of light.

He felt tingling all over his body as he went through, then emerged out on the other side.

Jack stood in the middle of a village. There were people bustling about, browsing for things on market stalls.

Tall red houses stood side by side. Jack could hear the haggling going on, people striking up deals for vegetables and meats. A chicken flapped off away from a cage. A flustered market-stall attendant tried to serve a customer.

Jack glanced back. Through the portal, he could see Yeye had got into bed and put a little blanket over his legs and a pillow over his eyes. Jack smiled at the familiar sight, then with a fizz the circle disappeared.

Jack felt something brush past him. It was a green boar! On the other side of the street Jack saw an even weirder sight. A red creature with six legs and four wings was trotting about. Jack did a double take as he realised the strangest thing about the creature – it had no head!

Then something touched his arm. "ARGH!" Jack jumped out of his skin, but it was only Monkey, who had appeared out of the coin that Jack was still holding. Monkey jumped onto Jack's back excitedly and then pulled on his earlobe.

"I'll be your guide," he said, jumping over Jack's shoulders.

Jack couldn't stop staring. Overhead he spied a gaggle of flying geese in a funny shade of pink. He recognised the Duoji, a wolf-like creature with red eyes and a white tail that featured in a story that

Yeye had told him. It was much bigger in real life. The geese started honking noisily as a large cloud went over the sun.

Jack glanced up. The cloud was growing, spreading out and getting darker by the second. It sped towards the village and swooped downwards. With a gasp Jack realised it was no cloud. It was a dragon! A real live dragon!

Jack's mouth fell open as it flew overhead. It was huge – probably as long as Jack's entire street – with a curving, snake-like body and long whiskers, blown back by the wind as it flew. The dragon's huge head whipped back and forth, side to side, as if it was looking for something.

As it passed overhead Jack caught sight of its huge claws, which looked more like giant eagle talons. It had no wings like the dragons in Jack's game, but as it moved through the sky as if it was swimming, its fish-like scales shimmering blue and silver.

As it flew, the dragon blew billows of white into the clouds. Snow flurries began to fall, lightly at first, and then heavier and heavier.

Jack stepped back to get a better look as the dragon circled overhead. It was the most incredible creature Jack had seen yet. This place was even more magical and amazing than Yeye had said! Jack put out his hand out to cup some of the snow.

It must be magical snow, he thought, as it wasn't a cold day and the trees were still covered in pink and white blossom. Just then, he noticed that the market vendors were hiding under their stalls. Families rushed into their houses. People were running, and Jack heard a baby screaming. The dragon had looped around and was on its way back, its huge jaws open. A woman holding the crying baby pushed past him.

"RUN!" she yelled. "Dragon attack! Run for your life!"

CHAPTER FOUR

The dragon swooped down low and breathed icy shards on to the market stalls. The fruit and vegetables froze like glistening baubles, then smashed as the stallholder knocked over the table in his rush to flee.

"Quick, this way!" Monkey raced over to a nearby haystack and Jack ran behind him, his heart pounding. *What was happening? Yeye had said it was safe!*

"Quick, call the others, Tiger Warrior!" Monkey said, jumping up and down on the spot, his arms flailing about.

"Um ..." Jack stuttered. "OK, I'll try." Crouching down, he fumbled to get the coin out of his pocket as he hid. The last thing he wanted was for the dragon to see him and turn him into an ice lolly.

Jack held the coin in his palm. Yeye had been the one to summon the animals and open the portal before; would Jack be able to do it? With trembling hands, Jack held the coin in his fingers. He flipped it up in the air and it twirled high.

"ZODIAC!" Jack bellowed. "Please work …" he added under his breath. In the blink of an eye, he was surrounded by all twelve animals. Jack gawped as he saw the animals he hadn't met before. There was a mighty horse with a chestnut coat and thick black mane. A small white rabbit darted near Jack's feet, diving into the haystack so that there was only a pair of concerned eyes peeking out. There was a snorting noise behind him, and Jack turned to see a brown ox the size of a small car, a glistening golden ring through its nose. But most amazing of all was the creature rising behind the ox. Another dragon. Like the Ice Dragon she had a long face, long whiskers and a serpent-like body covered in beautiful scales. But unlike the Ice Dragon, this one had red scales and a friendly face. She smiled at Jack.

"Don't worry, young Tiger Warrior," she said, "we've got your back. Animals … be prepared. You too, dear Rabbit." Jack punched the air like Yeye. Yes! He'd summoned the zodiac animals! But his excitement faded as they all looked

around at the chaos and destruction.

"What has happened?" Snake gasped
in dismay.

"Oh cool, a dragon fight! Come on,
Tiger Warrior, let's get it!" Rat grinned.

"What?" Jack gasped. "No way! I can't
fight a dragon!"

"You are the Tiger Warrior, whether you like it or not," said Rabbit from under the haystack.

"But Yeye said he would teach me. I haven't had any training yet!" Jack exclaimed.

"The Tiger Warrior needs to see the Jade Emperor at once," said Tiger.

Jack breathed a sigh of relief. In the stories Yeye told, the Jade Emperor was a great leader with god-like powers. He could fight a dragon, no problem.

"Baaaaaa but how are we going to get there?" Goat asked.

The zodiac animals looked at Jack expectantly.

Jack closed his eyes and banged his head with his knuckles. *OK,* he thought to himself, *think of it like a computer game. I have all of these animals, which are like power-ups...* "We need to get to the Jade Emperor's place. Didn't Yeye say one of you had the power of speed?"

"Me!" neighed Horse. "Get on to my back and we can be there in an instant."

"Too late," squeaked Rabbit, peeking out from Horse's shadow. The Ice Dragon had circled overhead and was bearing down on them, body straight like an arrow as it hurtled down towards them. "The Ice Dragon has seen us!"

"And she looks mean!" barked Dog.

Dragon took charge. "Everyone! Assume defence positions around Jack!"

"Sometimes being a small animal has its advantages! It's easier to hide!" said Rabbit, hopping further under Horse as the Ice Dragon's deadly breath burst out, freezing the haystack.

The dragon stretched out its claws as it swooped down, smashing the frozen straw into little pieces. Sharp shards of ice exploded everywhere like pieces of glass. The animals dived to the ground for cover. The haystack was gone, leaving Jack exposed. As the animals gathered themselves once more the Ice Dragon soared up into the sky.

"I've got it!" Jack gasped. "Snake, can you make me invisible? Then we can go to the Jade Emperor without the dragon seeing."

"Sure ..." said Snake, beginning to wind around Jack's arm. Jack's arm and half his body had disappeared when a dark shadow flew overhead. The Ice Dragon's piercing yellow eyes held Jack in their sights.

It opened its gaping mouth and darted down, speeding towards Jack. Snake was trying to make them invisible, but Jack's head was still showing.

Hurry, Snake, thought Jack desperately. *Make me invisible, quick!*

Just then, a bright ray of sunshine burst out from behind the dragon. And in it appeared a majestic, bird-like creature, the sunlight bouncing off its multi-coloured feathers. It looked like a peacock, but it was much bigger, and instead of being blue, its feathers were black, white, red, yellow and green.

It flew down, passing the Ice Dragon, darting this way and that. Then it turned, hovering in between Jack and the dragon. Snake uncoiled herself. Jack shielded his eyes from the sunlight that seemed to follow the magnificent creature.

"Whoa!" gasped Rat. The bird darted up, taking the fight to the Ice Dragon. Its

beak smashed into the dragon's chest
with such power that it knocked the icy
breath out of it. The bird whipped back
around, its feathers spread wide.
It spun in the air, its feathers
sending lightning bolts
of energy into
the sky. They
hit the Ice
Dragon, which
plummeted
down, nose-
diving towards
the ground. Just
before it hit the debris
below, the dragon twisted

and pulled up, freezing a row of trees with its icy breath as it flew away. A roar of anger groaned on the wind. The Ice Dragon had retreated, for now.

Jack and the zodiac animals surrounded the strange bird as it flew down to where they stood. Jack felt his whole body sag with exhaustion. That was close. Real fighting was nothing like computer games!

The bird was almost as big as Jack when it landed next to him, and its feathers were even brighter and more beautiful than they'd looked from below. It folded its wings over its face, then Jack watched in amazement as one by one as the feathers disappeared, and in their place stood a girl. She had dark hair and eyes, and was wearing bright green trousers and a gold top.

"That was so cool!" Jack gasped.

But the girl's face was blazing with anger. "Who do you work for? Is it the Dragon King?" she demanded.

Jack stepped back defensively. "The Dragon King? No. I'm— Well, I'm the Tiger Warrior."

"Nonsense! The Tiger Warrior is an old man!" The girl glared at him and raised her fists as if she was about to strike. Jack raised his own hands in surrender, trying to get her to understand he didn't want to fight her. Because if he did, he would definitely lose!

"You don't understand," he said, "that's my grandpa ... Tell her!" He turned to the animals, but to his surprise, none of them would look at him. And was Dog ... laughing? Jack stared at the animals. Ox let out a snort and Monkey was slapping his thighs and rolling around on the floor.

"Huh? What's going on?" asked Jack. Even the shy rabbit was tapping his feet with glee.

The girl patted him on the arm and he whipped round, ready for her attack.

But to his surprise she was laughing too. "I'm sorry!" she said. "I couldn't resist messing with you! I know you're Jack. Chonglin – your Yeye – said that he would soon be passing the Jade Coin to you. But he couldn't have picked a worse time." A shadow went over her face and she looked serious now. "Anyway, welcome to the Jade Kingdom," she said. "I'm glad you're here."

Jack gave a sigh of relief. The girl was as bad as Yeye, playing tricks on him! "You know all about me, but who are you?" he asked.

"I'm Li," the girl said.

"Princess Li," Dragon said. She bowed and Li scratched her behind the ears.

"My power is aligned with the Fenghuang – the bird you saw. My father is the Jade Emperor," Li continued. Yeye had told Jack all about the phoenix, and her amazing powers. He hadn't mentioned that she was a girl his age.

"Great!" Jack said. "The Jade Emperor can get rid of the dragon easily. Where is he?"

Another shadow crossed Li's face. "My father is missing," she said sadly. "There's no one to fight but us."

CHAPTER FIVE

Jack looked around at the devastated village in dismay. A few hours ago he was beating a dragon in a game and now he was meant to fight one in real life?

"I can't believe Chonglin passed the power over now." Li shook her head. "With him as Tiger Warrior we had a fighting chance. But now ..." She looked at Jack and sighed.

"Thanks," Jack said sarcastically.

Li waved her hand. "You know what I mean. Did he give you any training?"

Jack shook his head. He wished Yeye had taught him something – anything – before sending him into the Jade Kingdom. Even a flying kick would be helpful right now!

Princess Li nodded once, like she'd made up her mind. "Well, we don't have a choice. I can't do it on my own. Come on," she said, "let's get out of the open in case the Ice Dragon returns. Next time it might not be alone. I'll take you to my hideout. I really need your help."

Before Jack could reply, Li was already

striding off down the path.

"Hang on, are you sure this is the right thing to do? I mean, leave the village?" Jack asked.

"Yes, we need to regroup," said Li, speeding ahead towards the mountain. "And I'm starving after fighting that dragon."

"Me too." Jack suddenly realised his stomach was rumbling. "I don't suppose you have any fish and chip shops around here, do you?" he said, half joking.

"Chips? What are chips?" Li looked confused.

"Never mind," Jack said. "Tell me what the deal is with this Dragon King."

"My father, the emperor, imprisoned the Dragon King ten years ago," Li explained as they walked. "They were mortal enemies for centuries. The Dragon King upset the balance of Yin and Yang – Light and Dark. There have to be elements of both for harmony to work, but the Dragon King only wanted power. He used to be good and ruled the seas well, but that was not enough for him. He dreamed of taking over the Jade Kingdom and invading your world too, of being the supreme ruler of all the realms. There have been many Dragon Kings before him, like there have been many Tiger Warriors. But this one is the worst."

She gave Jack a look, and he didn't need Goat's telepathy to know she thought that he was the worst Tiger Warrior too.

"Look, I'm new to this. It's my first day as Tiger Warrior, OK? Everyone has issues on their first day." Jack tried to sound more confident than he felt.

"The first day of my job, I was made commander of Father's army and I vanquished thirty demons." Li said. "We have to fight. If the Dragon King takes over then the Jade Kingdom is done for – and so is your world. Our worlds exist side by side. The Dragon King won't stop until he has conquered all heavenly and earthly planes. At least you have the zodiac animals."

Jack rubbed the coin in his pocket. "The animals ..." he muttered. In a flash, the twelve animals appeared around him.

Tiger nudged Jack's elbow with his big furry head. Monkey scampered up on to Jack's shoulder and patted his back. And Rooster pecked at Jack's trainers, trying to eat his shoelace like a worm. Dragon tried to move Rooster out of the way with her tail, but Jack picked him up and stroked the jittery fowl. Even though Jack knew he was magic, he felt like a real bird in his arms.

"Don't worry, Tiger Cub, we'll all help

you," said Dragon. Jack felt better.

"Come on, we have to go," Li said, tugging on Jack's arm.

Jack looked at the zodiac animals. With all their power, why were they walking? "Li, let's get there quicker. You can fly and I can use Horse's speed."

"That's actually not a bad idea!" With that, Li spun in the air and turned back into the Fenghuang. She rose into the sky and flew, her beautiful feathers billowing in the wind.

Jack climbed on to Horse's muscled back and, as the other animals returned to the coin, they sped off like the wind, following the bright bird in the sky.

Li led them to
a tumbledown
wooden building at
the edge of town.
She landed and
returned to
her human
form. "I've
been hiding here
since the Dragon
King took over the
palace. It used to be
a tavern," Li said, opening the creaky
wooden door.

"Oh, like a pub," Jack said, looking
at the vines creeping up all around it.

The tables and chairs were covered in dust and had been moved to the side of the bar. At the back was a room full of wooden training equipment. Li gave Jack a bowl of leftover soup. There were noodles and beansprouts and some kind of purple spotty vegetable he'd never seen before floating in it, but he was so hungry that he ate it without complaint.

Jack looked at all the equipment as he ate. One object was shaped like a man but had wooden blocks stuck all over it. "What's this one for?" he asked.

"Practising hitting all parts of the body." Li ran over and began to attack it, using her hands to hit different areas all over the wooden man.

"Wow, that's amazing," said Jack. He watched as she hit each block hard. He wondered if he could have a go – but there was no way he could fight like Li.

"I've been training since I was three," she told him. "My father always told Chonglin to teach you, but he said you should have a 'normal' childhood. More normal than a princess with magic powers," she said, pulling a face. "But now you're going to have to learn how to harness the power of each animal on your own."

Jack's tiredness disappeared as he thought about using the animals' powers.

He took out the coin and was about to call an animal, when they all sprang out, chatting and bustling for space next to him. Li watched with amusement.

"Pick me, Tiger Warrior!" Dog barked excitedly.

"No! I'm going to be the most useful," Tiger roared.

"Dragons should fight dragons," interrupted Dragon, moving to stand between Tiger and Jack, her red scales shining in the light.

Rooster pecked the side of Jack's bowl. But greedy Pig shoved him out of the way. He was about to gulp down a leftover beansprout when Rooster pecked it out of Pig's mouth.

"Oi!" Pig began to chase Rooster around the training room. Rooster flapped and fluttered from beam to beam with the white tail of the sprout hanging out of his mouth like a worm. Finally, he settled on a rafter, flipped his neck back and swallowed the beansprout whole.

"Quiet, everyone!" Jack yelled. "I need to think." He turned the magical coin over in his hands. "So, I need to be touching the animal to use its power," Jack muttered to himself, remembering how Snake turned him invisible. "Rooster, come down from there. Let me see what you can do!" Jack said, laying his chopsticks parallel on top of his bowl. Pig grunted as Rooster flew down and sat on Jack's shoulder.

Jack held the coin in his hand. "ROOSTER," he yelled.

At first, nothing happened, but then Jack felt his feet lift up off the floor, slowly at first, and then faster until he was soaring up by the ceiling. Jack looked down at Li and the animals. This was amazing! He couldn't control his movements at all – and Rooster was flapping wildly – but he was flying! Jack zoomed around the room like a helicopter, then put out his arms like an aeroplane.

He was just starting to get the hang of
it when he began to sink lower and lower
towards the ground.

Rooster's powers were
fading!

"What's
happening?" said
Jack, confused.
"Why are we
landing?"

"Bok bok bok!"
Rooster replied.

"He said, until you can fully transform
into the animal, you can only control its
power for so long," said Rat as Jack's feet
touched the floor.

"Oh! Well, it was still fun!" Jack said to Rooster. "Tiger, you next!" he said. He was looking forward to harnessing Tiger's power. He didn't know what it was, but it was sure to be something cool!

Tiger nodded. "We should probably go outside to use my power. We wouldn't want to damage the princess's hideout."

They all went outside. Li followed, an amused smile on her face. Jack felt like he was being set up for another trick. Ignoring the sinking feeling in his stomach, Jack touched his shoulder to Tiger's flank and flipped the coin into the air. "TIGER!" Jack shouted. Instinctively, he held his hands out in front of him.

Jack felt a pulsating sensation and
then out of his palms flashed spheres
of fire. Unlike the rooster's power, he
wasn't struggling to make it work. He
felt comfortable with
this power, like he could
control it more.

He turned to Tiger with
an excited grin and Tiger
nodded.

"Not bad!" said Li with
a smile. "I was expecting to see you get
blasted on to your bum!"

They both laughed. And for a second
Jack felt like maybe he could actually
do this. Maybe he could defeat the Ice

84

Dragon. But then their laughter was interrupted by the sound of screaming.

"Come on! Let's go!" Li shouted. "The village is in trouble!"

CHAPTER SIX

When Jack and Li got back to the village it was worse than before. People were clambering over each other to leave with their belongings. Li was about to charge into the centre of the marketplace, but Jack held her back.

"Hang on – Li, I know you're a warrior, but shouldn't we wait?" *It's like in a computer game,* he thought to himself.

You don't want to enter the arena until you know what you are dealing with. "Let's just watch, until we know who we're fighting." He ducked behind a building and peered out into the marketplace. Li thought for a second, then gave a sharp nod and joined him. *Maybe she doesn't think I'm completely useless,* Jack thought.

They watched as a tall figure with a long, heavy robe and wild black hair strode into the village square. He was holding a glowing green staff with his bony fingers and his nails were long and yellow. He was followed by the Ice Dragon from before, and a smaller yellow dragon. Jack watched as it pulsed with electrical current that zapped out of its mouth and along its thick whiskers.

As they passed a fruit stall, the man gave a lazy grin and touched it with his staff. The stall exploded immediately, sending chunks of melon splattering over the marketplace. No wonder the villagers were scared. They didn't stand a chance.

"It's him!" Li whispered urgently. "The Dragon King! The staff is what's made him powerful enough to defeat my father. We have to get it!"

"Come out, you peasants!" the Dragon King yelled. "I want to know where the Fenghuang and the new Tiger Warrior are hiding. My Ice Dragon told me of their escapades earlier!"

Jack saw a man cowering behind a barrel. The Ice Dragon picked him up with one scaly claw and threw him on the ground at the Dragon King's feet.

"Well ... where are they?" demanded the Dragon King. He pointed the staff and the man rose up and hung in mid-air, his feet kicking to get free.

"I wouldn't tell you even if I knew!" the man said bravely.

"Ha!" laughed the Dragon King. "We'll see how brave you and your people are after you hear my demands. The Fenghuang and the Tiger Warrior MUST

come to my palace by sundown – or else I will imprison all of you, just like your beloved Jade Emperor!" The Dragon King lifted the staff and banged it on to the ground, releasing the man, who ran away. As a whirlwind began to swirl around the Dragon King, he pointed to the Electric Dragon.

"Destroy this puny little village!" he boomed, and disappeared.

"This is terrible!" exclaimed Li. "We have to do something, now!"

Jack looked around at the villagers, who were scattering in fear. "You're right, we can't let that Electric Dragon destroy the village. We need a plan ..."

Jack turned to Li, but she wasn't there.

She was running towards the Electric Dragon. It was firing pulsating electric currents that were blowing up houses all around it. The villagers screamed and ran for cover as rubble fell and fire spread. Li sprang into the air and with one quick twist, changed into her Fenghuang form. Her feathers fanned out in glorious colours, her claws sharp and ready for action.

"OK, I guess the plan is to jump right in there." Jack stared down at the coin. Which animal could help? If he used Rooster's power he could fly, sort of. Or maybe Tiger's fire? Then he remembered something that had been said earlier. Dragons should fight dragons ... Jack tossed the coin into the air, shouting out, "DRAGON!"

Instantly Dragon was by his side, ready to fight.

"What did you say your power was again?" asked Jack.

Dragon smiled. "My power is controlling water; it is the realm of dragons. That one over there destroying everything is under a curse. It is unnatural for a dragon to breathe electricity."

Jack bit his lip. He knew that water and electricity didn't mix; it was really dangerous. But maybe danger was exactly what he needed to fight an enormous dragon …

As his dragon moved her great head to look up at the sky, Jack followed her gaze up to where the Fenghuang was attacking the crackling Electric Dragon. But the dragon was just as strong. It sent out a current from its eyes towards the Fenghuang. The Fenghuang nimbly dodged one, then another, but the last attack pulse struck her on the side. She plummeted to the ground, hitting it with a thud.

"Li!" Jack called out. He and Dragon had to act fast. The Electric Dragon was diving towards Li. Jack placed one hand on the cool scales of Dragon's back and felt her power surge through him.

"Find a water source," Dragon told him calmly. Jack realised he could feel water nearby, cool and welcoming. He pulled his other hand up, and water rose like a sheet out of a nearby well. The Electric Dragon was walking towards the Fenghuang, its mouth open, ready to blast her.

"Li! Roll!" Jack yelled. Without taking a breath, the Fenghuang rolled away from the Electric Dragon. Jack threw his hand towards the Electric Dragon and a powerful jet of water shot out, cascading

down in a great torrent. The soaking wet dragon fizzled and made a popping sound, then fell to the ground with black smoke pluming out of its nostrils. Jack let go of Dragon and felt her power drain out of him.

They'd done it! He had done it! Jack stared at the fallen dragon. Maybe he could be a warrior after all! Li got up and in the blink of an eye was back in her human form, running towards the prone creature. She knelt hard on the yellow dragon's stomach.

"Where is my father?" she demanded. Jack ran over, Dragon close behind, ready to help if needed.

"OK, OK!" the yellow dragon cried, billows of smoke coming from its nose. "I'll tell you anything – just no more water. The Dragon King has imprisoned your father under the Mystic Mountain, in revenge."

"How do we free him?" Jack asked, hovering his hand over Dragon in case he needed to blast this beast once more.

"It is only the staff's powerful magic that holds him there." The Electric Dragon's head dropped to the floor. Jack thought the dragon was surrendering. Instead, it bent its head so its claw could touch a small purple jewel right in the middle of its forehead.

"What are you doing?" Li demanded.

Jack looked up as a sound rang out in the sky.

"Oh no! He's summoned the Ice Dragon, look!" shouted Li.

"I'm here!" Dragon touched her flank to Jack's side. But something in Jack said that it wasn't water power that he needed – after all, how could water fight against ice?

Think! he muttered to himself. Tiger had fire power, but that wouldn't work against the Electric Dragon ... and Li wouldn't be able to hold it down for ever. Jack knew he needed to harness the power that could take them both out.

Suddenly he had an idea.

"Sorry, Dragon, but I need someone else. OX!" Jack shouted as he flipped the coin. Dragon disappeared, and in his place stood a confused Ox, swishing its tail. "Did you mean to call me?" Ox said in her slow voice.

"Yes! Supreme strength, right?" Jack looked up; the Ice Dragon was close now.

"Jack! Hurry up!" yelled Li, struggling to hold the Electric Dragon down.

"I hope this works," Jack muttered to himself. He touched his foot to Ox's hoof, and felt his muscles firm up as super strength flooded his body.

"Li, on the count of three … let go of

the dragon and move out of the way."

"Are you crazy?" Li called. "If I let it escape we'll have two of them to fight!"

"Trust me, I've done it before," Jack said, not mentioning that it had been in a game. "The Ice Dragon won't want to hit its friend."

"OK, but if you ..." Li saw the shadow of the Ice Dragon overhead. "It's here!"

"One ... two ... three!" Li leapt off the Electric Dragon, who thought it was free. It twisted to its feet, but as the Ice Dragon approached Jack grabbed the Electric Dragon and held it in front of himself and Li, using it as a shield. The Electric Dragon twisted and pulled, but Jack had Ox's super strength pulsing through his arms and he lifted the enormous dragon easily. He felt like he could lift a whole city!

But Jack had made a mistake. The Ice Dragon didn't care about its friend. It opened its mouth so wide that Jack could almost count its spiky teeth, then roared out a bolt of its freezing ice power. The Electric Dragon screeched as the magical ice hit its scaly back, and its body shook in Jack's arms. Frost started appearing over its body from the head to the tail. The freezing cold burned Jack's hands until he couldn't hold it any more, and he let it go. The Electric Dragon smashed into a million little pieces of ice at his feet.

"I can't believe you did that!" Jack shouted after the Ice Dragon as it wheeled away. Jack brushed ice from his hands and blew warm air into his palms.

"One dragon down! One to go!" Li shrugged.

"OK." Jack held his hand up for a high five. But Li just stared at it. When she hesitantly held up her hand in the same way, Jack slapped it. "It's a high five! It means we did a good thing!"

"I don't think we should celebrate just yet," Li said, glancing up at the sky. "We still have one dragon to fight – and it looks very, very angry!"

CHAPTER SEVEN

Li was right. The Ice Dragon was coming for them, looking angrier than ever.

Li spun and transformed into the Fenghuang once more. She took flight, her wings open and ready for battle. She darted up and over the Ice Dragon, confusing it for a second. But Jack knew that to defeat the Ice Dragon they would need something that could battle ice.

Now was the time to bring out the ultimate fire power!

Jack flipped the coin and yelled out, "TIGER!"

Suddenly, Tiger was by Jack's side. "I'm ready," he growled.

Jack got on to Tiger's back and felt a heat in his hands. Fire power. It was back – and it felt so good!

"I'll attack from the top!" Li yelled, zooming into a loop the loop and soaring over the top of the Ice Dragon. She sent her lightning wing attack down on to the Ice Dragon's back, making it wobble in the air and slow down.

Jack got ready and aimed. Two fireballs

flew into the sky, but the dragon ducked out of the way. Jack's third flaming bolt sailed through the sky, narrowly missing the Fenghuang.

Jack gasped. "I'm going to hit Li by mistake."

"Don't think negative thoughts," Tiger growled. "We can do this together. Tap into your fierceness. Tell yourself, 'I AM THE TIGER WARRIOR!'"

"I AM THE TIGER WARRIOR!" Jack shouted. The Ice Dragon inhaled a huge breath and flew towards the village, ready to use its deadly ice power. It was now or never! Jack saw the point he wanted to hit on the dragon and aimed.

Two flame balls blasted
from his hands and Jack
and Tiger watched as
the fire flew through
the sky … and hit the
Ice Dragon square in the
chest.

The Ice Dragon exploded into a ball
of flames, then rain fell from the sky as
the dragon's icy body turned to water.
Li opened her wings and sent beautiful
firework-like colours
from the tips.
The Ice Dragon
had been
defeated!

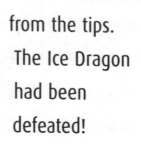

"We did it!" Jack exclaimed.

"YOU did it!" Tiger replied. "I told you, you are the Tiger Warrior."

Jack slid down from Tiger's back, and stood proudly by his side as the Fenghuang flew back down to the ground and returned to her human form. Doors creaked open slowly as the villagers who had been watching from behind their shutters crept out now the deadly dragons were gone. Then they began to bang their woks and ladles together, cheering their new heroes. Someone sent magical sparks shooting across the marketplace, and the air was lit up with tiny fireworks which zipped around before exploding in colourful bursts. The animals of the zodiac appeared out of the coin and surrounded Jack and Tiger.

"Who are you?" called a villager.

"He is the new Tiger Warrior!" Li told them. "Not bad for your first day on the job," she joked, giving Jack a little punch on the arm. Jack beamed a smile at her. He was glad he wasn't doing this all alone.

Monkey climbed around Jack's waist and held out his hand for a high five.

"Tiger, Dragon, Ox ... you did great. Thanks for lending me your powers!" Jack said as the smaller animals gathered around his feet.

"You did a great job – for a small warrior!" said Tiger.

"Your father would be proud of you today," said Dragon, bowing her great head so low that her whiskers almost touched the ground.

Jack gasped. "Of course – you knew him." His dad had been here, talking to the zodiac animals, just like he was now.

"We'll tell you all about him," Goat said, reading his mind.

Jack turned to face Li. She had a distant look on her face now as she stared at the Mystic Mountain.

"But my father ..." she said, pointing to the mountain, "is still trapped under there. This isn't over."

"What shall we do?" asked Rabbit.

"We have to go to the palace and break the Dragon King's staff. It's the only way to free my father."

"Li, wait," Jack said, grabbing her arm before she could transform. "Let's think about it for a second. The Dragon King doesn't know the two dragons are gone. If we can sneak in and steal the staff without a big fight we can break the spell holding your father and free him."

"Maybe. It's not a terrible plan," Li said hesitantly. "OK, you're on. I'll race you there!" She spun and flew up into the sky as the Fenghuang, her iridescent phoenix feathers shining as she flapped her wings. Jack flipped the coin once more.

"HORSE!" he shouted. Then together they sped away towards the Jade Palace.

Jack couldn't believe his eyes as they sneaked into the compound of the Jade Palace. The main building was huge, towering up into the sky. It was red, not green as he had imagined, and its roof had golden curved edges. Stone beasts guarded the entrance, along with guards who were now serving their new master. Li changed into her human form and Horse disappeared back into the coin as they ran through a side door.

"No one knows about this entrance," Li whispered as she led him down darkened tunnels, until they surfaced in a room full of ornaments. Jack's eyes widened as he took in huge scroll paintings and golden statues that were bigger than he was. Jade vases sat on top of small pillars.

"This is my father's collection. Many are gifts from people he has helped," Li said. "The throne room is through there. We need to be really quiet." Jack nodded.

They rounded a corner and saw the Dragon King sitting on the jade throne, two guards standing beside him. The staff was leaning against the throne.

The Dragon King
looked even more
menacing than
before, and as
he yawned
Jack could
see his teeth
were jagged
even in his
human form.

Li and Jack
watched from a distance as the Dragon
King talked to one of his guards.

"I'm going to fight!" whispered Li,
about to charge at the Dragon King.

Jack held her back. "Wait! I have an

idea. I'll try to grab it without being seen – I can use Snake's invisibility."

Jack could tell Li was still bursting to attack, but she gave a sharp nod. "I'll distract him."

"OK!" said Jack, hoping this was going to work. "SNAKE!" he hissed. Snake appeared and began coiling herself around Jack's arm.

"Are you ready?" asked Li, holding up her hand for a high five. Jack grinned and slapped her hand.

"Ready," he and Snake said in union. Snake wove around Jack's arm and he felt that strange melting sensation as his body vanished from sight.

Li walked slowly out of the shadow into the room towards the Dragon King, who was sitting on the throne, tapping his long fingernails. Jack tiptoed around the edge of the room, trying to avoid the probably priceless ornaments that stood on plinths all around.

"You shall release my father immediately!" boomed Li, her hands on her hips. The guards raced towards her, but the Dragon King waved them away.

"Ah, Princess Li. Come to surrender, have you?" The Dragon King laughed. Jack crept towards the throne, sneaking closer to where the staff was resting. He just needed to take a few more steps.

But he was struggling to control Snake's power and he could feel it slipping away.

Then Snake gasped. "Oh no … sssssorry, Jack," she hissed. Jack looked down at her, and saw his arm starting to reappear …

The Dragon King's head whipped round and he gave a wicked laugh as he saw Jack's body coming into sight. Snake wrapped herself tighter around Jack's arm, trying to keep him invisible, but it was no good.

"Uh oh!" Jack said as his whole body reappeared.

"Children, children. Such fun and folly you bring." The Dragon King laughed, showing his menacing teeth. "What a puny excuse for a Tiger Warrior you are. And I thought your predecessors were pathetic ..." He stood up, unfolding his tall, bony body from the throne. Jack joined Li in front of the Dragon King.

"Pathetic, eh?" Jack felt a flash of anger. No one called his family names! "My grandpa is brilliant. He put your lizard-butt under that mountain and you're going back there!"

"Silence!" the Dragon King spat. "You two are just weak children!"

"Weak children who defeated your dragons! They're gone!" Li said triumphantly. That got the Dragon King's attention. He raised an eyebrow, and for a second Jack thought that he looked worried. But then the Dragon King drew himself up to his full height and Jack saw that he wasn't concerned – he was furious.

"In that case I will have to KILL YOU MYSELF!" he roared. His body burst into a coil of black and green as he transformed into a gigantic dragon!

CHAPTER EIGHT

As the huge dragon towered over him Jack fumbled for the Jade Coin, almost dropping it. The Dragon King was four times the size of the other dragons that he and Li had defeated. His huge head had whiskers the size of anacondas. On his back, scales as black as charcoal provided thick armour. His eyes blazed red. He was like the ultimate enemy at the end of a gaming level; they always looked invincible and it took several attempts to beat them. But Jack and Li didn't have multiple lives.

Li jumped into the air and transformed into the Fenghuang. She circled and shot out her lightning bolts. They seemed like mere inconveniences to the massive dragon, hardly penetrating his thick scaly skin.

"TIGER!" Jack bellowed. He scrambled on to Tiger's back and began pelting the Dragon King with fireballs, but the dragon was surprisingly quick for his size, his snake-like body twisting and turning to avoid each fireball.

Suddenly, the Dragon King's tail swung
round, knocking Jack
and Tiger over. The
tail landed on Tiger,
and another claw
clamped down
hard over Jack. He
was trapped. Worst
of all, he was no
longer touching Tiger.
Jack gasped as he felt
Tiger's power drain out of him. He was
a normal schoolboy once more. Li flew
overhead and pecked at the claw that
held Jack prisoner, but it wasn't working.
She couldn't free him. She flew up to try

attacking from another angle. But it was no use.

Jack writhed and struggled under the claw, reaching out an arm towards Tiger, who was flattened by the great tail. But no matter how much he struggled, he just couldn't reach him.

The Dragon King laughed at him. *If only I could transform INTO Tiger,* Jack thought. But he didn't know how to. What had Yeye said to him before Jack stepped through the portal? That Jack had to harness the tiger's spirit. But what did that mean?

Jack closed his eyes and took a deep breath, trying to remember what Tiger had said to him. *Don't think negative thoughts. Tap into your fierceness. We can do this together.* Jack glanced at where Tiger was pinned, and saw him nodding.

"I am the Tiger Warrior. I AM the Tiger Warrior," he repeated, louder and louder. He imagined the fire of Tiger's power flooding through his veins and exploding out of his hands, how good it felt to have his hands flaming and shooting fireballs. How easy he'd found controlling Tiger's power. How he had been born in the year of the tiger, just like his father, grandpa and great-grandmother before him. How he was born to do this. For a second, it felt like he and Tiger were connected again. His fingers closed around the cool surface of the magic coin. Holding his breath, he flipped the jade coin.

"TIGER TRANSFORM!" he yelled. Jack felt the power of Tiger ripple throughout his cells, energy bursting from his head to his toes. He wasn't using Tiger's power. He WAS TIGER POWER!

Giving a roar, Jack burned with fire so hot that the Dragon King released him with a howl. As Jack padded past a huge vase, he saw himself reflected, a gigantic tiger whose stripes were flaming hot. Each step he took left fiery footprints on the floor. Jack bounded towards the

Dragon King and raked his claws down his back. The dragon shrieked with pain. His cry shook the pillars as he whirled around to face the Tiger Warrior.

The Dragon King lunged at Jack now, his claws slashing towards Jack's tiger throat. But Jack was powerful too. He leapt into the air and landed on the Dragon King's head, his flaming paws scorching the skin of the scaly creature. The Dragon King tried to fling him off, but Jack used his claws to cling on.

Li transformed back into her human body. She darted over to the throne, going for the staff. The Dragon King saw her out of the corner of his eye and whirled like a cyclone across the room to attack her. Jack was thrown to the floor. The Dragon King was almost upon Li when she shouted.

"Tiger Warrior!" she yelled as she threw the staff into the air. The Dragon King looped back around, trying to reach for the staff. Jack knew he had one chance. Suddenly he remembered the move Yeye had shown him at home. The flying kick! He growled as he leapt into the air, his tiger body twisting, his leg outstretched. The Dragon King's mouth was open to catch the staff, but instead Jack's flying kick connected with his jaw, sending him smashing into the wall. Jack caught the staff in his tiger teeth and slammed it into the ground, shattering it with an almighty bang. It splintered into a thousand shards. With the staff's power gone, the Dragon King returned to his human form, crumpled in the corner.

Jack felt the tiger power drain out of him as he returned to his regular body. Then the walls of the Jade Palace began to shake.

"It's an earthquake," he yelled. "Come on, let's go!"

But Li was smiling. "It's not an earthquake ..." She grinned. "It's my father. He's coming home!"

CHAPTER NINE

The tremors shook the throne room so
fiercely that Jack could barely stay on his
feet. A zap of lightning hit the throne,
filling the room with thick black smoke.
When the smoke cleared, the throne
wasn't empty any more! An old man
with a thin beard lifted up his shoulders
and opened his eyes. When he saw Li
he smiled. He looked regal in his silken

green robes, and his face looked tired, but even a few days imprisoned under a mountain hadn't dampened the Jade Emperor's power. He stood up tall and opened his arms.

"Come here, my child!" he said.

"Father!" Li cried out as they hugged.

Then the Jade Emperor's expression darkened as he looked at the Dragon King, still lying crumpled on the floor. "Come!" he commanded. Jack watched as the Dragon King stumbled towards the Jade Emperor, and was surprised when the Dragon King dropped to his knees.

"Forgive me," the Dragon King said, holding up his hands for mercy.

"I fell for that once. Never again," said the Jade Emperor. "Back to the mountain for you."

But the Dragon King had been holding back. With one last scathing look at Jack and Li, he clapped his hands together and disappeared in a puff of smoke.

"Shall we go after him, Father?" asked Li.

The Emperor shook his head. "He has gone where we cannot follow – to the spirit realm. But he is bound to try once more to take over the Jade Kingdom, and the worlds beyond. When it is time to face him again, we must be ready."

The Jade Emperor turned and looked at Jack as if noticing him for the first time.

"So, it seems we have a new Tiger Warrior," he said.

"Yes sir, your highness, sir ... majesty ... sir." Jack bowed his head.

"Your ancestors will be proud of your actions today," the Jade Emperor said. Li was still scowling about the Dragon King's escape. "I don't know why we can't banish the Dragon King for ever, Father, especially after

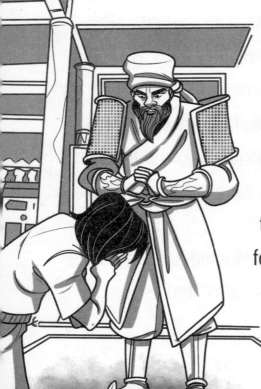

he killed Ju-Long—"

Jack gasped, a chill running through his body like an electric shock. "The Dragon King killed my dad?"

"Didn't you know?" Li asked, looking horrified.

Jack shook his head numbly.

"Yes, your father was killed by the Dragon King," said the Emperor. Jack felt his insides flip.

The animals of the zodiac beamed out of the coin, as usual glowing in many colours. Dragon tried to comfort Jack. Rabbit stroked his foot, Dog rubbed against his leg and Monkey put one long arm around Jack's shoulders.

Jack felt his face harden with grief. He would learn to harness all the powers of the zodiac animals – and then, one day, he would get revenge for his father's death.

As if reading his mind, the Jade Emperor shook his head. "You show much promise, young Tiger Warrior. But you must train hard and focus on being a good team with the Fenghuang, rather than thinking of revenge. Revenge is what drives the Dragon King. You do not want to become like him." He clapped his hands suddenly, making Jack and Li jump. "But for now, I think it is time for you to return home."

Jack nodded. He would train hard and look after the Jade Kingdom ... but one day the Dragon King would pay for what he had done.

"Thank you for helping me. All of you," Jack said to the animals and to Li.

"Bye, Tiger Warrior." Li held her hand up for a high five. Jack gave her palm a slap. The Jade Emperor raised his eyebrows.

"It's how you celebrate in Jack's world, Father," said Li. Then she bowed to Jack. "And this is how you say goodbye in mine."

Jack bowed to Li and the Jade Emperor and then flipped the coin. "HOME," he said, just as Yeye had told him, what felt like a lifetime ago. The portal opened and Jack stepped through.

Yeye's room was just as Jack had left it, full of Yeye's cartoons and his bowl of mints. Yeye was still asleep in his bed, snoring loudly.

How strange to be home after having such an amazing adventure, thought Jack. He felt in his pocket to check that it wasn't all a dream, that he did in fact have a magical coin that opened portals to other realms.

Suddenly, Rooster appeared, flapping and squawking all over Yeye's bedroom. Yeye sat up in bed, his eyes wide from the commotion.

"Jack! Yeye!" Mum called from the hallway. As quickly as he could, Jack flipped the coin and said "ROOSTER!" – and just as Rooster disappeared the door opened.

"What's going on?" Mum asked suspiciously, eyeing Yeye's room. A softly glowing feather fell to the floor, and Jack kicked it under the bed.

"Nothing!" both Yeye and Jack said together.

"Yeye was going to play a computer game with me," Jack said quickly.

"Strange, I'm sure I heard a ... chicken or a duck or something." Mum looked around suspiciously, then walked out. Yeye got out of bed and shut the door behind her. His face was bubbling with anticipation as he ushered Jack over to the bed to sit down.

"Tell me everything! How did you like your little holiday in the Jade Kingdom? The egg tarts are to die for! Am I right?"

Jack sat on the edge of the bed. Where should he begin? He leant over and squeezed Yeye's arm tight. "You'll never believe what happened. The Dragon King escaped and sent two killer dragons to destroy a village. The Jade Emperor was

imprisoned and the Fenghuang and I had
to break the staff. Then I remembered I
had to harness the power of the tiger and
you had shown me the flying kick earlier
on ..." Jack stopped to catch his breath.

"Slow down, slow down!" Yeye gasped.
"The Dragon King came back? And you
fought him?"

"Yes! I thought we were going to be
toast and I'd never see you again. I kicked
butt, Yeye! I became a tiger just like you."

Jack explained everything about
harnessing the tiger's power at just the
right time, Yeye's eyes lighting up as he
listened. At the end Yeye laughed and
slapped his thigh.

"Well, you are a true Tiger Warrior. The heart of a tiger and the power of a dragon ... even though you still have the body of a schoolboy!" Yeye laughed.

Jack remembered something else. "I know about Dad ..." he said, sadly.

Yeye grew serious. "I'm sorry I couldn't tell you before," he said. "He died bravely. And he'd be so proud of you, Jack. But you still have a lot to learn. No doubt, some day you will have to face the Dragon King again."

"I'll be ready," said Jack, looking into Yeye's eyes. "I promise!"

THE END

For fun activities and more about Jack and the Jade Kingdom, go to:

www.orchardseriesbooks.co.uk

Look out for the next Tiger Warrior adventure,

THE WAR OF THE FOX DEMONS!